DISCARD

GEORGIA'S TERRIFIC, COLORIFIC EXPERIMENT

ZOE PERSICO

RP|KIDS
PHILADELPHIA

This is Georgia.

She comes from a family of fantastic artists.

Her mother, father, brother, and grandma leave Georgia
in awe of everything they create.

Even the family dog has some creative ideas.

But Georgia is special.
She dreams of being a scientist!

From the vastness
of the cosmos

to the cell structures of
plants and animals,

she is fascinated by science.

Georgia loves studying the works
of famous scientists, too.

She is captivated by Marie Curie's studies
on radioactivity.

She admires Galileo Galilei's discovery of gravity.

She fawns over Isaac Newton's conclusions about the color spectrum.

One day, Georgia has an idea.

"I've read countless studies and handfuls of hypotheses, but I have never created my own unique experiment. If I can do that, I am sure to be a great scientist!"

"Need any help?" her mother asks.
"I can show you how to sketch out your plans."

"No, thank you."

"Let me give you a few tips,"
her father states. "I think adding some color
could really enhance your scientific findings."

"That will NOT be necessary."

"I don't know, Georgia, you need
a pop of visual awesomeness," her brother says.
"I can show you how to sculpt something amazing."

"ENOUGH!
I don't need any help. I am not an artist.
I am a scientist! Science is about proper calculations
and not silly imaginative ideas!"

"Fine!" her brother says. "Don't be like us.
Go ahead with your fancy schmancy calculator, books, and beakers.
Hopefully, your experiment doesn't BORE you too much."

"Since my science-ness seems to be boring you,
I can be found in my SCIENCE hut alone!"

With a leap in her step, Georgia packs everything
she can and leaves the house. Past the garden and
through the gate, she runs into the woods.

Georgia can finally begin her experiment
and be a TRUE scientist!

At first she is having
the most extraordinary time,

but she then has some trouble getting started.

"I can study the color spectrum!
But this has been done before."

"What about how gravity works?
Wait, this has been done before, too."

"I'll create my own radioactive material!"
Georgia says. "But that's not original
or safe, is it?"

Georgia sighs. She'll need to come up with her own ideas to create something special. Georgia has the motivation, but where's the inspiration?

"How do scientists come up with such amazing experiments? What am I missing?"

But then an idea strikes!
"How does my family get creative?"
she wonders.

Georgia tries something new—
something that's not from her library.

COLOR
WHEEL

3.14

It feels odd for her at first, but with every colorful beaker
she fills and each new shape she draws, her excitement grows.

It is time to head home.
Georgia makes her way back.

"What do you want? Rubbing your boring science in our faces?" asks her brother.

"I want to show you all something," Georgia says.

"Science can be a work of art, too."

Georgia's mom smiles.
"I bet you can teach us some fun science facts
that will help us with our art."

Georgia smiles back. "And I bet you can give me
some great art tips so I can invent more
beautiful experiments."

This is Georgia the scientist and her family of fantastic artists.

They used to work separately, but now together they create sculptures, paintings, and experiments that leave everyone in awe.

Even the family dog helps out. Georgia and her family agree:
with art and science working in harmony, inspiration never runs dry.

FOR MOM, DAD, TIERNEY, AND SHAE.
YOUR PASSIONS INSPIRE THIS ARTIST EVERY DAY.

Running Press Kids
Hachette Book Group
1290 Avenue of the Americas, New York, NY 10104
www.runningpress.com/rpkids
@RP_Kids

Printed in China

First Edition: April 2019

Published by Running Press Kids, an imprint of Perseus Books, LLC,
a subsidiary of Hachette Book Group, Inc. The Running Press Kids name and logo
is a trademark of the Hachette Book Group.

The Hachette Speakers Bureau provides a wide range of authors for speaking events.
To find out more, go to www.hachettespeakersbureau.com or call (866) 376-6591.

The publisher is not responsible for websites (or their content)
that are not owned by the publisher.

Print book cover and interior design by Frances J. Soo Ping Chow.

Library of Congress Control Number: 2018935979

ISBNs: 978-0-7624-6524-8 (hardcover), 978-0-7624-6525-5 (ebook),
978-0-7624-6590-3 (ebook), 978-0-7624-6589-7 (ebook)

1010

10 9 8 7 6 5 4 3 2 1

3